The Heroes of White Whale Lighthouse

Written by Alison Milford

Illustrated by Adam Horsepool

Collins

It was a wet day at White Whale Lighthouse.
Amy and Pete waved at their dad and Philip,
the lighthouse keepers.

"Stay inside," said Dad. "It's very windy."

By the evening, a storm raged across the sea.

"That's strange," said Amy. "Why is
the lighthouse lamp not on?"

Pete spied a ship sailing close to White Whale Rock.
"We must tell Dad!" he cried.

They rushed across the bridge to the lighthouse.
Giant waves crashed around them.

At the lighthouse, they searched for
the lighthouse keepers.

It was empty.

The keepers were not in the kitchen.

"Where could they be?" whispered Amy.

"Perhaps they're trying to fix the lamp," said Pete.

The top of the lighthouse was empty too.
Pete lit the lamp.

The light lit up White Whale Rock.

"Phew!" said Pete. "The ship is safe."

"But Dad isn't!" cried Amy.

Amy and Pete rushed down to their dad.

"We came out to see the ship and the wind pushed Philip onto the ledge!" he cried.

They grabbed the rope and pulled Philip to safety.

Suddenly there was a loud noise! The ship's mast snapped.

"We have to save the crew!" cried Philip.

"What can we do?" asked Amy.

"Get the house ready," replied Dad. "They'll be very cold."

The lighthouse keepers rowed out to fetch
the ship's crew.

The wind howled. The giant waves whooshed.

Whoo!

Whoosh!

The lighthouse keepers saved all the crew.

Soon the ship sank beneath the waves.

Amy and Pete helped the crew get dry.

Can I have some porridge, please?

The skipper gave Amy and Pete a little ship in a bottle.

"Thank you," he said, "for helping us!"

"And for being the best lighthouse keepers of White Whale Rock," added their dad.

How did Amy and Pete help?

 After reading

Letters and Sounds: Phase 5

Word count: 300

Focus phonemes: /ai/ a /ee/ e, y, e-e /oo/ u /igh/ ie, y /ch/ tch /j/ g, ge, dge /l/ le /f/ ph /w/ wh /v/ ve /s/ se /z/ se

Common exception words: of, to, the, said, do, were, their

Curriculum links: Science: Light

National Curriculum learning objectives: Reading/word reading: apply phonic knowledge and skills as the route to decode words, read other words of more than one syllable that contain taught GPCs; Reading/comprehension: drawing on what they already know or on background information and vocabulary provided by the teacher

Developing fluency

- Your child may enjoy hearing you read the book.
- Read the first double page, demonstrating how to read with lots of expression. Encourage your child to read the sentences ending in exclamation marks with emphasis and to read **Whoo!** and **Whoosh!** on page 17 to sound like the wind and sea.

Phonic practice

- Focus your child on the care they must take in sounding out -se endings. Can they pronounce the /s/ or /z/ sounds correctly in these words?

  house   please   noise   heroes

- Repeat for words ending in -y. Check your child understands how "y" is used to make the /igh/ or /ee/ sound in these words:

  Amy   windy   by   empty   safety

Extending vocabulary

- Ask your child to think of an antonym for each of the following:

  rushed (e.g. *walked slowly, dawdled*)   whispered (e.g. *yelled, shouted*)

  crashed (e.g. *trickled, stroked*)   safe (e.g. *in danger, in peril*)

  empty (e.g. *crowded, full*)   loud (e.g. *quiet, soft*)